The Elephant

WITHDRAWN

Peter Carnavas

pajamapress

Canada Council Conseil des arts
for the Arts du Canada

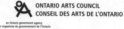 ONTARIO ARTS COUNCIL
CONSEIL DES ARTS DE L'ONTARIO
an Ontario government agency
un organisme du gouvernement de l'Ontario

Canadä

The publisher gratefully acknowledges the support of the Canada Council for the
Arts and the Ontario Arts Council for its publishing program. We acknowledge the fi-
nancial support of the Government of Canada through the Canada Book Fund (CBF)
for our publishing activities.

Library and Archives Canada Cataloguing in Publication

Title: The elephant / Peter Carnavas.
Names: Carnavas, Peter, 1980- author.
Description:"Originally published by University of Queensland Press, Queensland,
Australia,
   2017."--Title page verso.
Identifiers: Canadiana 20190159960 | ISBN 9781772781021 (hardcover)
Classification: LCC PZ7.1.C37 Ele 2020 | DDC 823/.92—dc23

Publisher Cataloging-in-Publication Data (U.S.)

Names: Carnavas, Peter, 1980-, author, illustrator.
Title: The Elephant / Peter Carnavas.
Description: Toronto, Ontario Canada : Pajama Press, 2019. | Originally published
by University of Queensland Press, Australia, 2017. | Summary:"A young girl named
Olive imagines her father's depression as an elephant that follows him everywhere
he goes. Determined to rid her home of the oppressive elephant, Olive gets help
from her grandfather and her best friend with an expression of love that helps set her
father on the path to recovery"— Provided by publisher.
Identifiers: ISBN 978-1-77278-102-1 (hardback)
Subjects: LCSH: Mental illness – Juvenile fiction. | Families -- Juvenile fiction. |
Love – Juvenile fiction. | BISAC: JUVENILE FICTION / Social Themes / Depression &
Mental Illness. | JUVENILE FICTION / Social Themes / Emotions & Feelings.
Classification: LCC PZ7.1C376El |DDC [F] – dc23

Original art created with ink
Cover and text: based on original design by Jo Hunt

Manufactured by Friesens
Printed in Canada

Pajama Press Inc.
181 Carlaw Ave. Suite 251 Toronto, Ontario Canada, M4M 2S1

Distributed in Canada by UTP Distribution
5201 Dufferin Street Toronto, Ontario Canada, M3H 5T8

Distributed in the U.S. by Ingram Publisher Services
1 Ingram Blvd. La Vergne, TN 37086, USA

For Bron, Sophie, and Elizabeth

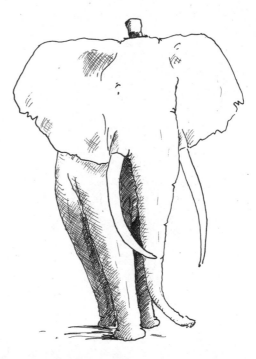

The Elephant

When Olive walked into the kitchen, she found an elephant sitting beside her father at the small wooden table. They both wore the same weary expression and stared out the window, as if it were a painting they had never seen before. The elephant's shadow filled the room with darkness and it wore a small, black hat.

"Hi, Dad," said Olive.

Her father swung his head away from the window and looked at her with raincloud eyes.

"Hi, honey."

A frown fell upon his face. "Why are you wearing your bike helmet?" he said. "I haven't fixed your bike yet."

Olive smiled, hoping the smile might be contagious.

"Well, it's only a bike helmet when I'm riding a bike," she said. "I'm going to climb my tree, so today it's a tree helmet."

Her father nodded and turned back to the window. The elephant sighed.

Olive left them cocooned in the kitchen. She opened the back door and stepped outside.

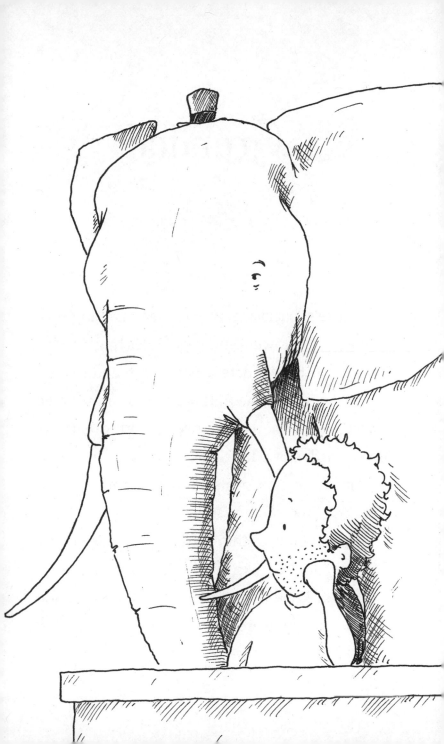

Grandad

Olive's backyard was a neat rectangle of grass, with flowers and vegetables hugging the edges. A thin concrete path stretched toward a rusty clothesline and a giant jacaranda tree stood near the back fence, covering half the yard with slow, dancing shadows. A tire swing hung from one of its branches and a round trampoline stood nearby.

Olive loved the yard, though it hadn't always looked like this. Once it had been a mess of knee-high weeds, and the jacaranda had barely flowered.

That was before Grandad moved in.

He was in the garden now, hunched down in the pumpkin patch as Olive skipped across the grass toward the tree.

"Heya, Olive!" he called.

He straightened up and Olive thought he looked like a skinny scarecrow, his old, straw hat full of holes.

"Hi, Grandad," she said. "How are the pumpkins?"

He wiped the sweat from his forehead with a dirty hand.

"You could ask them yourself," he said.

Grandad was always telling Olive to talk to plants.

"You've got your helmet on," he said. "Has your dad fixed your bike?"

Olive shook her head. She felt something brush her legs and she looked down.

It was Freddie.

He was a small, gray dog with short legs and an extra-long tail.

She bent down and scratched him behind the ears.

"No," she said. "He hasn't fixed it yet."

Then she ran to the tree.

The Thinking Spot

Olive started to climb.

She needed to wear her helmet today because she was going to one of the higher branches, to her thinking spot. Hand over hand, foot over foot, she scrambled up and nestled into a comfy nook.

She looked up.

There was a tiny speck in the sky, high above the town. It was a bird in the shape of the letter V, like a fine pencil mark in the sky.

How might the town look from up there, from the wings of that bird? It would be something like a storybook town, a toy village. Olive pictured it all as a tiny patchwork quilt, the roofs of the houses like colored squares stitched loosely together. She imagined the thin, gray roads weaving between the blocks of houses like fine cracks in eggshell. The trees would billow and breathe like tiny puffs of deep-green cloud and the backyards would look no bigger than the fingernails on her hands.

She watched the bird until it became smaller and smaller, a dot in the sky, and then so tiny that it seemed to disappear, as if it had become part of the air itself.

How could something be so light? Olive's gaze drifted back down, down to her own backyard. Her eyes settled on her house and the kitchen window.

All the lightness fell away as she thought about the elephant.

The big, gray elephant that shadowed her father.

It hung over him at breakfast.

It trudged beside him when he left for work.

At night, it lay by his side, weighing everything down.

Every day she saw that elephant.

And, every day, she wished it would go.

Just then, there was a sharp yap. Olive snapped awake from her thoughts and looked down to the bottom of the tree. There was Freddie, his long tail standing tall, his watery eyes gazing up at her.

Arthur

The next day was the beginning of a new school term. Olive sat at her desk beside Arthur. He was a small boy with curly hair and dark brown eyes. Those eyes were usually focused on the pages of an enormous book— *Amazing Facts About Frogs,* or *Everything You Need to Know That You Don't Know Already*— but sometimes Arthur's eyes would sparkle and dance, when he told a story or flipped around the playground.

Olive liked Arthur most of all because she could tell him anything. Anything at all.

"An elephant?" he gasped. "In your house?"

She nodded.

"But—how? What?" Arthur blinked hard. "What do you mean?"

Olive's eyes swept around the classroom as the children sharpened pencils and rummaged through their desks.

"It's a bit hard to explain," she said. "It follows my dad around. Whenever he looks sad, I see the elephant there."

"Doing what?" said Arthur.

"Not much," said Olive. "Just there, making everything really heavy and really hard for my dad."

The other students had settled into their desks and their conversations softened to a gentle hum around the room.

"How long has it been there?" asked Arthur.

"As long as I can remember."

"And you've never told me?"

"I'm telling you now. Besides, I wasn't sure if you would believe me."

Arthur shook his head. His eyebrows bunched together. He spoke between blinks.

"I believe you, but—well, is it real?"

Olive leaned a little closer to Arthur and lowered her voice.

"Well, that's the thing," she whispered, but she couldn't say any more for Ms. March had started talking to the class.

Ms. March

"Good morning, children," said Ms. March. "I hope you all had a lovely break."

Ms. March was a thin, cheery woman who seemed to move whichever way the breeze blew. A clutter of jewelry hung around her neck and plastic earrings like small hula hoops dangled from her ears. Her hair was a delightful mess, an orange nest of tangled twirls and curls, with ribbons and clips and flowers springing out, as if trying to escape the knotted jungle.

Her desk was much the same.

It was piled high with books, folders and stacks of paper, pencils and pens, calculators, and counting blocks. There was probably a tennis ball under there somewhere, a floppy sun hat that she would fish out for playground duty, and a jar of wilted flowers balanced on top of it all. She could never find anything she wanted, and this amused the children endlessly.

"This term, we're going to share some very important things with each other. But first— does anybody know how old our school is?"

Olive and Arthur looked at each other and shrugged.

"Anybody?" said Ms. March.

A tall boy with big ears edged his hand into the air.

"Um, I don't know how old it is, but I know it's really old," he said.

"How do you know that, Kyle?" said Ms. March.

"Because Mr. Briggs has been teaching here his whole life and he's about a hundred years old."

The students broke into laughter until they saw Ms. March wearing her unimpressed face, though Olive spotted a smirk curling at the edge of her mouth.

"Cedar Hills Primary School—not Mr.

Briggs—is turning one hundred years old this year," said Ms. March.

The children smiled and raised their eyebrows at the mention of such a big number.

"Therefore," she took a deep breath, "we will be having a school birthday party at the end of term."

This time, cheers and applause filled the room. Ms. March waited for silence.

"As the school is now very old, we will be studying old things—the old things in our own lives and in our own homes. At the end of term, at the birthday party, we will present them to the school community."

She fluttered to the side of the room.

"Now, I've brought something to get us started." Her eyes were wide and her voice soft, as if she was sharing a secret. "It's old— and it's wonderful."

The children lifted themselves just slightly off their chairs to watch as Ms. March stood beside something that was leaning against the wall, covered in a blanket. Olive hadn't even noticed it was there.

The teacher clutched the blanket, ready to whip it off and unveil the surprise.

"This is something from a long, long time ago," she said. And as she lifted the blanket, the children gasped and whispered through their smiles.

"It's a bike!" one of them declared, as if the others hadn't figured it out.

But it wasn't an ordinary bike. Just as Ms. March had said, it was old and wonderful.

"This was given to me by my father," she said, "and it was given to him by his father. That means it's very, very old."

The children were invited to take a closer look, to trace their fingers along the cracked paint on its frame and pluck the rusted spokes as if they were harp strings.

"We'll all be sharing things like this in the next few weeks." Ms. March tapped the handlebars and she gazed at the bike with glassy eyes. "I want you to start thinking about the things your own families have, the old and wonderful things that make up the stories in your lives."

Looking at the broken, old bike, Olive knew exactly what she wanted to bring.

Lunch

At lunchtime, Olive and Arthur sat beside the handball courts. Arthur frowned at his jam sandwich, then peered into Olive's lunch box. She had a stack of colorful containers, each hiding something delicious: fruit salad, swirly yogurt, and homemade butter biscuits.

"I wish your grandad made *my* lunch," Arthur grumbled.

Olive smiled and spooned some yogurt into her mouth.

Arthur nibbled the crust of his sandwich.

"Do you know what old thing I'm going

to bring?" he said. "My dad has this really old instrument. You squeeze it in and out and it plays funny sounds. I'm going to bring that."

A sparrow bounced before them, pecked at a crumb and flew away.

"I want to bring my bike," Olive said. Her face was still, her eyes far away. "If my dad ever fixes it."

"Doesn't your dad fix cars?"

"Yes," she said. "He's good at fixing things for everyone else. But not me."

Arthur dropped his sandwich back into his lunch box. He started picking at the bruises on his apple.

"Um, Olive," he said, edging his words out carefully. "Can you tell me more about the elephant?"

She faced him and looked at his big, brown eyes.

"Can anybody else see it?" he asked.

Olive held her spoon still in the air.

"No. Only me." Her voice was full of quiet wonder as she spoke. "See, my dad has this really big sadness. He's had it for a long time. And I imagine the sadness is like a big, gray elephant following him around. That's what I see."

"Like an imaginary friend?"

"An imaginary enemy," she said.

Arthur took a bite from his apple. "And is it there every day?"

"All the time," she said, and then she couldn't stop. "He can't do anything when the elephant's there. That's why he doesn't pack my lunch. That's why he doesn't mow the yard. And that's why he'll never fix my bike."

The two friends sat silently after that. Most of the other children had snapped their lunch boxes shut and scurried off to the playgrounds and the oval, like a flock of birds suddenly taking flight.

At last, Arthur stood up.

"Do you know what I think?" He held his half-eaten apple like a microphone. "Your dad won't fix your bike—until you fix your dad."

Olive scrunched up her nose. "How do I do that?"

"Easy," said Arthur, crunching another bite from his apple. "Get rid of the elephant."

She laughed, because she suddenly realized three important things.

Arthur was weird.

Arthur was right.

Arthur was the best friend in the world.

The Bicycle

Later, at home time, Olive lingered outside the classroom when the other children had gone. She knocked on the door and stepped carefully toward Ms. March's desk. It was so quiet without any children in the room.

"Hello, Olive." Ms. March shuffled through the mess on her desk. "I'm looking for—have you seen that—oh, never mind."

"Ms. March," said Olive, "could I look at the bike one more time before I go?"

Ms. March stopped shuffling papers and smiled. "Of course."

Olive crouched before the old bike. The chain was clogged with rust. The stitching had come away from the seat. The paint had flaked off most of the frame, but she could see that it had once been a beautiful, burned orange. It was certainly old and broken, but it must have been something wonderful when it was young, when it was alive. It was like looking at a fossil and imagining the marvelous creature it had been.

Best of all, it was just like her own bike.

Side by Side

Grandad waited for Olive at the school gate. He wore his old scarecrow hat and his purple backpack was slung over his shoulder. Olive knew what that meant. She walked faster.

"Hi, Grandad," she said, throwing her arms around him.

"Hello, love."

"Where to, today?" she said.

Grandad leaned his whiskery face close to hers. "Secret."

Ever since Grandad moved in, he had taken over all of the ordinary, everyday jobs like packing lunch and cooking dinner. Things like that. He seemed to enjoy it and, anyway, Olive's father was always too busy at work or looking out the kitchen window. The best part about having Grandad around was that he sometimes did unordinary, not-so-everyday things. Like today. That's what the purple backpack was for. Whenever Olive saw it, she knew Grandad had something exciting planned.

"Can you give me a clue?" she said, skipping beside him along the footpath.

"Nope," he said.

For every loping step he took, she took four of her own.

"Can you tell me how far it is?" she asked.

"Not far."

Then Olive remembered the old song that she and Grandad loved. It was called "Side by Side" and they often sang it when they walked home from school. "How many 'Side by Sides' will it be till we get there?" she asked.

Grandad thought for a moment. "About five, I think."

They started singing as they walked. Each time they finished the song all the way through, Olive counted on her fingers. After once through, they were a block and a half away from school. After twice through, they were passing the corner store that sold their favorite milkshakes. And when they had sung it five times, they reached the cricket oval.

"Ah," said Grandad. "Here we are. Five times through. Just as I thought."

Olive's face went blank as she looked at the empty field. "Cricket?" she said. "We're going to play cricket?"

Grandad fanned himself with his scare-crow hat.

"Not quite," he said.

They walked across the oval, climbed over

a metal railing and made their way up a grassy hill.

Then they sat down.

From here, they could look down on the oval and see the whole town stretching away before them. Olive wasn't quite flying on the wings of a bird, but everything still looked very small.

"I used to bring your mum here when she was your age," said Grandad.

Olive swallowed hard. Her throat always went lumpy when Grandad talked about Mum. "I didn't know Mum played cricket," she said.

"She didn't," said Grandad. "We did this instead."

He pulled a piece of paper out of the backpack. He folded it this way. And that. Until he held in his weathered hands a perfect paper plane. He stood up and threw the plane.

It glided over the railing toward the center of the oval, slicing a straight line through the air, like a fish shooting through the sea. It flew on and on, so still and so swift at the same time, until it finally landed near the middle of the cricket pitch.

Olive's mouth had fallen open into a smile.

"It just kept going and going," she sighed.

Grandad smiled and rested a hand on her head. "Your turn," he said.

Together, they folded a piece of paper this way. And that. And, at last, Olive held the beautiful white plane in her hand.

"Go on, then," said Grandad. "Fly away!"

Olive stood and sent it soaring across the oval. It sailed a smooth arc over the grass, finally resting just a few feet from the first plane.

She laughed a bit at the simple beauty of it all—the white paper, the elegant arc, the soft green grass; and beside her, the purple backpack, Grandad's golden-straw hat, the sky a pale-blue umbrella embracing the whole town.

She tried to imagine her mother here, as a young girl standing on this hill. Her small hands folding paper this way and that, then shooting a plane across the oval. Did she leap and laugh just as Olive had this afternoon?

It was hard for her to picture her mother so young.

It was hard to picture her mother at all.

The Photograph

Later, at home, Olive lay on her bed. Freddie wrestled with an old sock beside her, tossing it into the air as he rolled on his back.

She reached for the framed photograph beside the lamp.

It was a photo of her parents.

Both of them.

In the photo, her father had his arm around her mother and his other hand shoved in his jeans pocket. He was smiling so much that you couldn't really see his eyes. They were all squinty. Olive hadn't seen him smile like that, with squinty eyes, for a long time.

Her mother wore a white hat that looked like it was about to blow off just as the photo was taken. She wasn't looking at the camera. She was looking at Olive's father as if he was more important than anything else and there was an ocean full of secrets that only they shared.

A year after the photo was taken, Olive arrived. And a year after that, her mother was gone.

Olive let the frame lie on her chest and wondered what a picture of her father would look like today. No smile. No ocean full of secrets. Just her father and the elephant squashing itself into the frame.

She blinked away a tear and noticed that Freddie was at her feet. His head was low, buried in the blanket on the bed, and he growled the way he always did when he knew Olive was sad.

Under the Bed

"Knock, knock."

It was Grandad outside Olive's door.

"Are you okay?" he asked.

She let him in and Freddie scampered under the bed. Grandad spotted the photograph in Olive's hand.

"Need cheering up?" he said.

She nodded.

"Come on, then," he said. "Tell me something about school today."

So she told him that she needed to find an old and wonderful thing to show the class.

"I want to take my bike," she said.

"Ah," said Grandad.

He nodded slowly. Olive knew the bike was special for him, too.

"That's your mum's old bike," he said. "A beautiful thing."

"I know," she said, twisting the corner of her blanket. "But Dad hasn't fixed it. He took it to his workshop and I haven't seen it since."

"Well," said Grandad, his eyes big and bright. "I have something else you might like."

The Typewriter

It sat on a rough, wooden desk at the front of the house, in the room they called the sunroom. It was black with freckles of rust. The keys were small and shiny and round, like little saucers perched on metal arms. All you had to do was push down one of the keys and a tiny metal hammer would fling forward and punch the ink ribbon, stamping that letter onto the page. It all happened with cheery, mechanical noises and Olive's favorite noise was the bell that sounded when you edged nearer the right-hand side of the page.

Ding! it said. *You're running out of room!*

All she knew of the typewriter was that Grandad had owned it for most of his life. Now she was about to find out more.

"This typewriter kept me close to your mum," said Grandad, with a faraway look in his eyes.

"What do you mean?" she said.

"Well, your mum loved poetry. When she grew up and moved away from home, I used to type out her favorite poems and send them to her. I could have just bought her a book of poems, but there was something special about typing them on the typewriter—she knew I must have read them and typed them the way they were supposed to be set out. It was something we shared."

Olive ran her fingers over the keys, then noticed Grandad dabbing his eyes with a handkerchief. She climbed on to his knees and wrapped her small arms around him, squeezing him tight.

Dinner

At dinner, Olive sat opposite her father and the elephant. She had Arthur's words running through her mind. *Your dad won't fix your bike until you fix your dad.* But Olive didn't know where to start. The best plan she had was to talk, to tell him about the old and wonderful things and why she needed her bike fixed more than ever before.

"How many cars did you fix today?" she said.

Her father chewed slowly. "Just one," he said, "and a half."

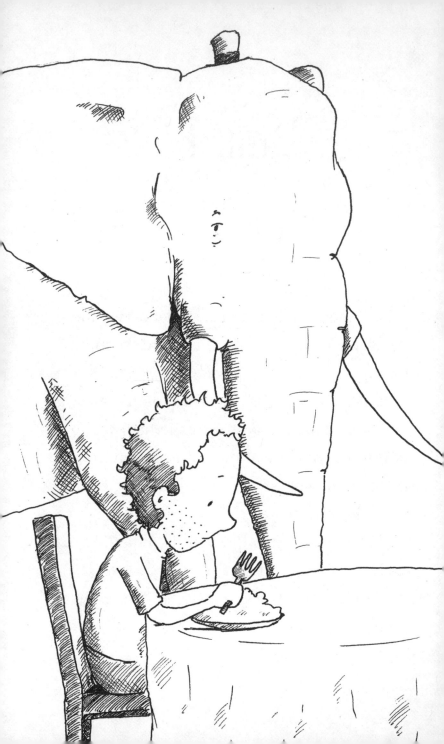

More chewing.

Olive tried again.

"Ms. March showed us a bike today," she said.

This time he glanced up from his plate.

"It was really, really old," she said. "Everything was rusty and the paint was peeling, but it still looked amazing."

He nodded, then looked back down and kept chewing.

One more try. "We have to take something old and wonderful to school," she said.

She glanced at Grandad. He raised his eyebrows and nodded for her to keep going.

"I really want to take my bike—Mum's old bike."

Her father rested his fork on his plate.

"Are you still fixing it?" she asked.

He rested his chin on his fist and looked at her.

She waited for him to say something. Waited for him to talk about the bike, the shape of the frame, the color of the seat.

She waited for him to look at her as if there were secrets that only they shared, if not an ocean full then at least a cupful.

She waited for the dirty, gray elephant to take off its hat, apologize, and disappear out the door, into the night.

Instead, her father said nothing and went back to his dinner. The elephant breathed heavily through its trunk.

Olive felt Freddie nudge her feet beneath the table. She patted his furry head and remembered the other advice Arthur had given her.

Get rid of the elephant.

Then she whispered to Freddie so that only he could hear, "How am I supposed to do that?"

The Squeeze Box

A few days later, Ms. March sat on the edge of her cluttered desk.

"Now, children," she said. "Before we present our old and wonderful things at the school's birthday party, we're going to take turns presenting them to the class. So, I'd like to write down what you're all planning to bring."

One by one, the students named their important things.

An old telephone.

A watering can.

A pair of binoculars.

A treasure map. (Ms. March raised an eyebrow but wrote it down anyway.)

It was Olive's turn.

"A bike." She looked down and scratched her knee. "I hope."

Ms. March moved on to Arthur.

"Well," he said, fumbling with something under his desk, "I've brought it along today."

Before Ms. March could say anything, Arthur was standing before the class. He held a strange box-shaped thing with hexagonal sides and his face was a picture of goofy pride, as if he were showing off a baby brother. He cleared his throat louder than necessary. A ripple of giggles swept through the class.

"This is a squeeze box," he announced, holding it out for all to see. "It's a box," he said, "and you squeeze it."

There was another flutter of giggles.

Arthur pressed some buttons on the side of the box and squeezed it in and out. A blaring, wonky noise blasted the room. It sounded like a wobbly chorus of busted car horns and the children's giggles turned to squeals of laughter.

Some of them fell off their chairs, or pretended to. Some, like Olive, nearly lost their breath, cackling, snorting, and banging the desk. Arthur played on, laughing himself, but he tried to look serious by closing his eyes.

"Very good, Arthur," Ms. March called over the noise, though she was red-faced and breathless, too. "What can you tell us about it?"

"It's my dad's," he said. "But it's really my grandma's. She used to play it at parties, I think, but she doesn't play it much anymore."

"Why not?" somebody shouted.

Arthur scanned the children with his dark, brown eyes, as if the answer might be written on one of their faces.

"Um," he said, "maybe she just hasn't been to a party in a while."

Then he gave the squeeze box one final blast, and the class erupted again.

The Book

"That was fantastic," Olive told Arthur as he slipped back into his desk. "I mean, you played it badly, but it looked great."

Arthur laughed as he clipped the instrument back into its case.

It was Quiet Reading Time. Olive fished a tattered novel from her desk and began flipping through the pages. Ms. March insisted on silence, but most of the children still carried on hushed conversations because she was usually under her table looking for something.

"Has your dad fixed your bike yet?" Arthur whispered, turning toward Olive.

She shook her head.

"Elephant still there?"

She nodded.

Arthur glanced over his shoulder, then pulled from his desk the biggest book Olive had ever seen. He held it up so she could read the title.

The Big Book of Elephants.

He heaved the book onto his desk. Olive tried to read her own book, but her eyes kept flicking back toward Arthur. He turned the pages and whispered to her as he read, keeping his eyes on the book. His voice fizzed with energy.

"Elephants are the biggest land mammals in the world," he said. "They keep growing their whole lives—up to thirteen feet tall and as heavy as ten tons."

Olive swallowed. Her throat stung. Her father's elephant was only going to get bigger.

"Elephants can live up to 70 years," Arthur continued.

She buried her head in her hands. It would be here forever.

He kept reading and whispering facts. With every bit of information, he suggested a way for Olive to get rid of the elephant in her life.

"Elephants eat bark and grass and leaves," he said. "Why don't you tempt it out of the house with a big, juicy branch?"

She smiled at the idea.

"They like mud baths," he said. "You could push it into that swamp behind the school."

She giggled.

"I know!" he declared, forgetting he was supposed to be whispering.

Ms. March peered at him from behind

a bookshelf. He waited until she turned away.

"Why don't you dress up as a lion? Lions sometimes attack elephants if they're really, really hungry."

Olive laughed, imagining herself with a tangled mane and sharp claws, jumping out in front of her father.

"It would definitely surprise my dad," she said to him, "but I'm not so sure about the elephant."

"I know," he said with a shrug, and Olive knew he understood. If it was any old elephant, these ideas might just work.

But her father's elephant was different.

It didn't eat leaves.

It didn't take mud baths.

And while her father was sad, nothing could scare it away.

The Pigeon

That afternoon, Olive ran to the gate and hugged Grandad. He carried his purple backpack again and Olive asked him where they were going this time. He refused to give her any clues and even resisted singing "Side by Side." Olive sang it secretly in her head, and after eight and a half times through they stopped at the entrance to a big patch of bushland. A sign read *Cedar Hills Nature Reserve* and Olive realized she had been here once before on a school excursion. All she remembered from that day, though, was a goanna that had scampered up a tree and a boy called Tyler getting a leech stuck to his leg.

Hand in hand, Olive and Grandad stepped into the reserve. The ground was damp under their feet and Olive breathed in the sweet smell of rotting leaves and decaying logs. Birds chirped and screeched somewhere among the trees, but Olive couldn't see them. Grandad let his hat slip off and hang down his back. Olive noticed his head was constantly moving, scanning the canopy, studying the undergrowth, as if his eyes were cameras trying to capture every detail of the place. She started to do the same, not knowing what she was looking for but hoping she would see something anyway.

They walked on, following the track that wound through the trees. They could have been anywhere in the world, lost in a tunnel of branches and leaves. The school, the town,

the elephant—they were all so far away. Hidden in this forest with her grandfather, side by side, Olive felt safe.

Grandad stopped.

So did she.

He put a finger to his lips, signaling her to stay quiet, but his eyes were fixed on something else, something up high. In slow motion, he peeled off the backpack, unzipped it, and took out a pair of binoculars. He used them to look at the top of the trees. After a few seconds, his old face creased into a smile.

"Olive," he whispered, still peering up through the binoculars. "Do you know what pigeons look like?"

"Yes," she said. "Small, gray things. Dad calls them rats with wings. They're ugly."

Grandad crouched and handed her the binoculars. He pointed up, through overhanging leaves, at a high branch. "Through there," he said.

She stared through the lenses and saw nothing but green. Then something moved. She focused on that spot and waited. It moved again and suddenly she saw it clearly. A bird, a great, bulking lump of a bird, round and plump, with a slender neck and beady eyes, and the most beautiful colors she had ever seen—rich greens, golden yellows, and, on its belly, a striking, deep purple.

"What is it?" she asked.

"A pigeon," said Grandad.

"But...it's so big," she said. "And it's beautiful."

"I know," said Grandad. "This one's called a wompoo fruit dove."

Then he patted her shoulder. "Just remember—they're not all gray."

Still gaping at the bird, she nodded.

Old Movies

The weeks passed and nothing changed. Olive watched her father lurch through the door every afternoon with the elephant lumbering beside him. He did the same thing each day. He put his wallet on the fridge. Drank a glass of water. He kissed her on the head.

The elephant followed him, without a sound.

It reminded Olive of old movies, the ones Grandad had played for her—black and white. And silent.

Some days, she asked her father about the bike. Some days, she talked about other things—anything.

But most days, like today, she said nothing.

She watched her father's routine—wallet, water, kiss—then ran outside with Freddie.

The Colorful Parts

Olive bounced on the trampoline, landing on her knees, back to her feet, then belly. Feet, back, knees, feet.

She jumped higher, stretching her arms to reach the jacaranda flowers hanging above. When she jumped this high, she could see a small plant growing in the gutter of the roof. She had seen it a week before but promised herself never to tell anyone, in case they pulled it out.

She slid off the trampoline, strapped on her helmet, and climbed the jacaranda.

Once again, she made her way to the topmost branches, to her thinking spot.

She looked down at the yard, at her world, and thought about her mother. Grandad always said her mother was looking down on them and she wondered if this was what she saw.

The circle of the trampoline.

The rectangular backyard, colored green.

The scruffy blob of Freddie, stretched out on the grass under the tree.

Everything looked neat and colorful from up here, but life was a bit gray and untidy once you were down there; once you climbed down the tree and shared the house with an elephant.

She hoped her mother could only see things from up high. And just the colorful parts.

The Record Player

One night, Grandad sat on Olive's bed as she drew scribbly thoughts onto a sketchpad.

"I need to take my old thing to school next week," she said.

Grandad peeked at the sketchpad. There were pictures of birds and an elephant and purple flowers. A bicycle was drawn in the middle of the page.

"Still not fixed?" he said.

Olive shook her head and started to rub out her drawings. She dragged the eraser across the page, cutting the elephant in half.

If only it were that easy.

"Come on, then," said Grandad, rubbing his palms together. "I have something else you might like."

It was a chunky, brown box with knobs and dials and a plastic lid on the top that flipped open. Under the lid was a big, round platform,

a perfect circle about the size of the clock that hung in Olive's classroom. There was a curved arm beside the circle, with a needle pointing out the end. Olive watched Grandad slide a round, black disk out of a plastic sleeve. It was a vinyl record and it looked like you could use it as a frisbee. Grandad studied both sides of the record, as if he were checking his reflection, then placed it on the round platform and lifted the curved arm. The platform started spinning around. He cradled the arm in his fingers and the needle hovered over the whirling record. Then he gently lowered the needle.

It made a soft crackling sound as it landed on the record, then moments later—music.

Beautiful sounds filled Grandad's little room: violins, clarinets, a tinkling piano.

The melodies floated and swam around Olive, and the room felt brighter and more colorful. The tiny needle followed its path along the spinning record and soon a voice joined the music. A woman's voice, sweet and smooth.

Olive sat cross-legged in front of the record player, watching the needle and listening to the words that poured out of the speakers.

Suddenly, her face beamed and she met Grandad's gaze.

His eyes twinkled.

"I know this song!" she announced. "It's 'Side by Side!'"

And it was. It was slower than when she and Grandad sang it, but the words were the same. She hummed along, and when the song finished, she asked him to play the record again. And again. And again.

Upside Down

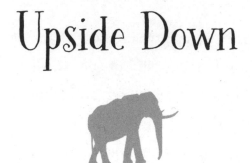

Olive and Arthur were on the monkey bars in the playground, hanging upside down.

"When's it your turn to bring something to school?" Arthur's arms and curly hair were falling toward the ground.

"In a few days," she said, dangling her arms.

"The bike—" Arthur said. "Has your dad—" He didn't need to finish. Even upside down, her face answered everything.

"What will you bring?" he said. "Do you have anything else?"

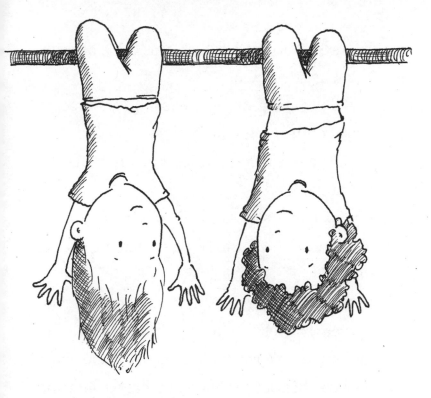

"Well," she said, "my grandad has lots of things—an old record player."

"A what?"

"A record player," she said. "It plays music. And he has a typewriter."

"A what?"

"A typewriter. You use it to type letters or stories or whatever."

Arthur nodded, which was a bit difficult, being upside down.

"So, which one?" he said. "The record player or the typewriter?"

Olive shrugged, which was even harder than nodding.

"Neither," she said. "They're more special to Grandad. I want to bring something special to me."

Arthur reached for the monkey bars and heaved himself up to sit on top. Olive did the same. Above them, giant shade trees swayed, their leaves and branches waving and overlapping. Small specks of the bright sky appeared and disappeared among the leaves. They looked like tiny stars in the daytime.

"There's a big tree in our backyard," said Olive. "Maybe that could be my old and wonderful thing."

Arthur stared at her. Then he burst into

laughter. "A tree?" he squealed. "How are you going to bring *that* to school?"

Olive laughed, too. He was right. How could she bring the jacaranda to school?

But then she had an idea.

The Camera

There was only one camera in the house. It belonged to Olive's father. There were strict rules about it, but Olive was running out of time for rules. So, that afternoon, she waited until Grandad had lost himself in a crossword, then tiptoed into her father's bedroom.

She crept over to the shelf that held the camera. As she reached for it, the small collection of other things on the shelf caught her eye.

An old book with crumbly, yellowed pages.

A handful of silver coins.

And two photos. Both of her mother.

In the first one, her mother sat at an outdoor table with a coffee cup in her hand, laughing at the camera.

The other one was her mother holding Olive as a baby, much the same way Arthur had held his squeeze box before the class.

That was all.

There were no pictures of Olive in her school uniform, or jumping on the trampoline, or riding her bike.

It was as if her father only wanted to remember the things that she couldn't remember at all—her mother and the ocean full of secrets. He was trapped in that time, and since then life had just become one big elephant.

She grabbed the camera and slipped out of the room. Freddie followed her, wagging that long tail of his.

"Grandad," she called. "Just going out to the backyard."

"Okay," he said. "But be careful. It's a bit windy out there. And take your helmet if you're going to climb the—"

The back door slammed. She was gone.

The Tree

Olive stood on the grass and aimed the camera at the jacaranda. If she couldn't take the tree to school, this would be the next best thing. She pressed the button and snapped a photo. Then another. She checked the pictures.

The tree only just fit into the frame. It was beautiful, of course, but it looked so small, so far away in that little rectangle on the display screen.

She took more photos, close-up shots of the flowers and the speckled trunk. She craned her neck back, looked up, and took pictures of the twisted branches stretching to the sky. She pointed the camera down and captured the gnarly roots that wormed and buckled in the grass, creeping away from the trunk. The colors leaped back at her through the little screen—the green grass, pale brownish trunk, the soft lavender of the flowers.

Her face was full of color, too, as she danced around with the camera, capturing the different parts of the great, hulking tree, all the beautiful pieces that combined to form this huge thing that towered over the yard.

Then she started to climb.

If she wanted to show Ms. March and the class how big and old and wonderful this tree really was, she would not only have to show them what it looked like, but what it felt like, too—to sit in its highest branches and get lost in those velvety clouds of jacaranda flowers.

She reached her thinking spot and looked down at the yard. She freed her arms from the branches and held the camera in front of her.

A breeze whipped by.

The branches shook.

And Olive fell.

Black

She landed with a thump on the grass.

Coughed and gasped like a broken-down car.

The sky reeled above her.

The branches warped.

Freddie whimpered and licked her face.

Then everything went black.

A Voice

"Olive. Are you awake?"

It was a deep, croaky voice.

"Olive."

A slow, tired voice.

Olive opened her eyes.

Blurry shapes.

Fuzzy blobs of color.

Was she under water?

She blinked and her eyes started to clear. She was in her room. In bed. But everything was swirling around her—the walls, windows.

"Olive," said the tired old voice. "It's me."

She turned to the voice and saw someone, or something.

She ignored the swaying wallpaper and focused on the thing in front of her, the owner of the voice.

Then she saw it. A tortoise. An enormous, gray tortoise, blinking sad, watery eyes.

"Olive," it said. "Can you hear me?"

Then she closed her eyes and went back to sleep.

Awake

There was the smell of toast, the soft song of a distant bird, and Olive woke up.

Morning sunlight leaked through the curtains, warming the foot of her bed.

How long had it been since she fell? A day? A week?

She pushed herself up onto her elbows and looked around her bedroom. The walls were no longer moving. Everything was still.

And there was the tortoise, a withered look on its ancient, gray face. Beside it sat Grandad, a coffee cup in one hand, a piece of toast in the other. In the morning light, he suddenly looked very, very old. He dropped his toast and rushed to her, wrapping her up in his scarecrow arms.

"I'm so sorry," he said. That old voice belonged to him and not the tortoise. Olive felt him shudder as he spoke through small sobs.

"It was too windy. I should have given you the helmet. I should have stopped you."

They held each other tight.

"I'm okay, Grandad," she said. "I'm okay."

"It's just," he sniffed, "when I found you— on the ground—I thought—" He gulped for air. "It felt like losing your mum all over again."

Olive held him tighter than she had ever held anything before. She glared at the big, gray tortoise in the corner of her room and understood perfectly.

Grandad had a heavy sadness all his own.

A sadness as heavy as a tortoise.

And it was all her fault.

Crumpled Paper

When Dad arrived home he poked his head into Olive's room and found her sitting on the floor, surrounded by crumpled balls of paper.

"You're awake," he said. "How are you feeling?"

Olive forced a smile. "I wish I could remember how to make a paper plane."

He sat on the floor beside her. The elephant squashed itself into the room, too.

"The doctor came," he said. "You've got a concussion. Just have to rest some more and you'll be fine."

"Okay." She nodded.

"Can I have some paper?" Dad said.

She handed him a piece and watched him fold it this way. And that way. And this way again.

But all he made was a folded mess.

"Grandad's really sad, isn't he?" said Olive.

Her father nodded.

"I know it's because of me," she said. "Because I fell out of the tree. It reminded him of Mum."

Her father turned his folded paper over and over in his hands. It looked so small in those big hands. They were used to fixing cars, not folding paper.

"The main thing is that you're okay," he said. "And don't worry about Grandad. He'll be fine."

Olive tossed and caught a ball of paper. She tossed it again, but this time it landed on

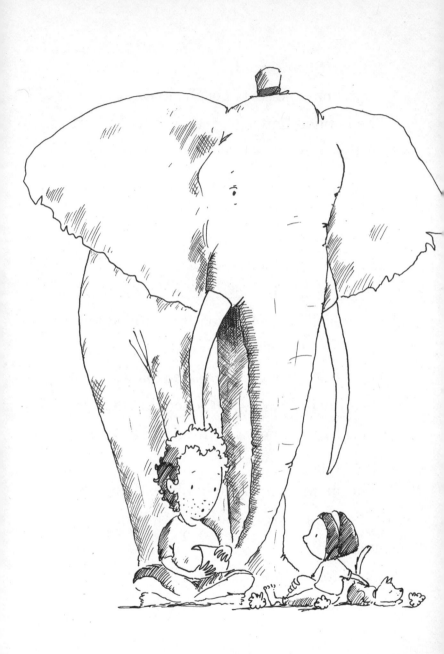

Freddie and woke him up. "Well, he can't walk around with that big tortoise for the rest of his life."

Wait.

Did she say that out loud?

Her father shot her a puzzled look.

She *had* said it out loud.

"Tortoise?" he said. "What tortoise? You feeling okay?"

Olive blushed. "Um, I think so." She wished she could swallow up her words. "It's just—I think—I wish there was something I could do."

Her father stood up. He seemed to have forgotten about the tortoise.

"I know you want to help," he said, "but it's hard to change the way people feel."

She knew that. Of course she did. She'd watched her father drag that miserable elephant around for so long and nothing was going to change that. But Grandad was different. Grandad threw paper planes onto the cricket oval. He found beautiful birds hiding in the forest. Grandad filled her days with color.

"He's the best scarecrow in the world." Oh no. Words had slipped out again.

Her father looked at her as if there were something wrong.

"You'd better hop back into bed," he said.

Olive climbed in and slid under the sheets.

"And remember," he said. "Don't worry about Grandad."

But Olive *was* worried. He wasn't supposed to be tied to a tortoise.

She had to think of something.

The Picture

"James brought in a sewing machine," Arthur whispered during Quiet Reading Time.

His words tumbled out so fast, it was as if they were chasing each other out of his mouth.

"Reyna brought her dad's old watch. Somebody brought in a school bag from about a hundred years ago. I think it was Ella. Except it wasn't actually a bag—it was more like a suitcase. Imagine bringing a suitcase to school every day."

It was Olive's first day back at school since

her accident. She had been away for a whole week, so Arthur was telling her about all the old and wonderful things she had missed.

"The best was Sam's—he brought in a mandolin. It was like a tiny guitar with eight strings. And his uncle actually came in and played it. I wish I'd brought Grandma in to play the squeeze box."

When Quiet Reading Time had finished, Ms. March skipped to the front of the room. It was time to share some more things that were old and wonderful.

"Olive," she said. "Lovely to have you back. Feeling better, I hope?"

"Yes, Ms. March," squeaked Olive, sinking into her chair. At least thoughts weren't slipping out anymore.

"You were going to bring an old bike. Is it here?"

Olive watched the teacher's orange curls

coil in and out. Her hula-hoop earrings danced about and her necklace clinked softly.

"No," she said, picking at a fingernail. "My dad hasn't fixed it. I was going to share my tree, but—"

Ms. March's face became quite still. It all came to rest—the hair, the jewelery—and her voice was gentle and direct when she spoke, as if Olive was the only other person in the room.

"That's fine," she said. "I'm sure you'll have something ready for the party."

Olive sat a bit straighter and nodded. Arthur flashed her a best-friend smile and his eyes shone.

He had *The Big Book of Elephants* on his desk, still there from Quiet Reading Time. Olive could see a photo of a giant elephant plodding along a dusty track with a baby elephant by its side. Their shadows were long and dark, but they didn't seem sad. There was something perfect and peaceful about the picture. It was lopsided but beautiful at the same time. One elephant weary and wise; the other young and full of trust.

When the rest of the class packed up, Olive didn't move. Her gaze was still fixed on the picture.

An Idea

Later that day, Olive and Arthur were upside down on the monkey bars again. Olive let her hands hang loose so they nearly touched the ground. She closed her eyes. Her thoughts somersaulted in her head, bumping and rolling into each other: the elephant, the tortoise, and the photo in Arthur's big book.

Like soft pieces of clay, these thoughts rolled around, then merged together to form an idea, big and bold and exciting.

"I've been thinking," she said.

"Uh-oh."

"It's about my old and wonderful thing. I didn't have one today, but I still need to bring something to the school's birthday party."

"You're not going to bring that tree, are you?"

She laughed. "No. I've thought of something else. But I need your help."

"Okay."

"Well—mainly your grandma's help."

Arthur narrowed his eyes. "My grandma?"

"I need her at the party." Olive folded her arms and nodded. "You did say she hadn't been to a party for a while."

Arthur scratched his curly hair and grinned.

"Does this have something to do with the squeeze box?" he said.

She gave him a thumbs-up, which looked like a thumbs-down when you were upside down, but he knew what she meant.

Happy Birthday

The night of the party arrived.

As the sun dipped away from the town and the stars opened in the sky, hundreds of children and their families funneled into Cedar Hills Primary School. Balloons bounced from the classrooms, streamers flapped around the buildings, and fairy lights sparkled along every path. There were enormous *HAPPY BIRTHDAY* signs lining the walls and many of the teachers and children were dressed in old-fashioned clothes—bonnets and top hats and shiny bow ties.

Olive trotted through the gate with Grandad and his tortoise. Her father was working late and wouldn't be coming. She pointed at the decorations as they walked, but Grandad looked up only once or twice. The tortoise was slowing him down. The colors and lights passed him by.

They entered the hall, where the school concert band honked out a few tunes while

everybody found their seats. Grandad folded himself down into one of the small, plastic chairs. The tortoise plonked beside him. Olive hugged Grandad and then joined her class near the front of the hall. She sat beside Arthur.

"Does anybody else know what you're going to do?"he said, his dark brown eyes very wide.

She tried to hide a smile.

"Not even Ms. March," she said. "Is your grandma ready?"

Arthur pointed to a lady sitting in the shadows beside the stage, a squeeze box on her lap.

"I've never seen her so excited," he said.

The evening began with a line-up of important-looking people saying important-sounding things. Some of them spoke too close to the microphone, so the children cupped their ears. Some of them forgot to turn the microphone on at all.

The important-looking people sat down and it was time for the class performances. The younger children went first, stomping and fumbling around the stage to the crowd's delight.

Then Olive's class was called up.

Her heart thumped inside her chest.

An Old and Wonderful Thing

The children stood in a row on the stage and Olive was last in line. Each student took a turn to step forward into the spotlight and talk about their old and wonderful thing.

A tennis racket.

A fancy watch.

A strange, skinny skateboard.

Arthur's turn came and instead of the squeeze box, he held up an old book, crumbling at the corners. Whatever he said about it made the crowd laugh, but Olive hardly listened; all she could hear was her pounding heart.

Her body quivered. Her teeth chattered.

She wasn't sure if she could do this.

She looked beside her and noticed a door open to the oval outside.

She could run. Just run out the door, across the oval and home to Freddie.

"Olive," somebody hissed. It was Ms. March crouched in front of the stage. "It's your turn."

Olive stepped into the spotlight. There was a sound, a sweet musical sound, which seemed to be getting closer. Everybody in the hall turned to face the edge of the stage as Arthur's grandma sauntered up to join the children. A gleaming smile stretched across her face as she nursed the old squeeze box in her hands. She pressed buttons and squeezed the box in and out. It filled the hall with beautiful chords and it was hard to believe this was the same instrument Arthur had squeaked and honked on just a few weeks earlier.

The microphone shook in Olive's hand. "This is a song my grandad taught me," she said.

Arthur's grandma stood beside her, bumping the music along with the squeeze box.

Olive began to sing.

It was a quirky, little song—old and wonderful.

It was "Side by Side."

Another Old and Wonderful Thing

With each line in the song, Olive's voice grew stronger and louder. Her hand stopped shaking. Her knees stopped clunking together. As she sang, she noticed all the tiny things that happen in a crowd when people enjoy themselves: their hands tapped out the rhythm, their bodies rocked from side to side, their eyes shone like tiny raindrops in the darkness of the hall.

By the final verse, Arthur was suddenly beside her, bopping along to the song as if they were old sailors chanting at sea. He slung his arm around her shoulder and pretended he knew the words. All he really managed to sing, though, was the final line, and some of the audience belted it out as well.

The applause that filled the hall was deafening. It sounded like a plane coming in to land on the roof. Olive had never heard anything as loud.

She spotted Grandad, perched on his plastic chair at the edge of the hall. A proud grin had spread across his entire face. His eyes were so sparkly and watery that small drops trickled down his cheeks, finding a home in his wrinkles, the way fresh rain tracks its way into dry riverbeds. It was the happiest he had looked since Olive's fall and it was hard for her to imagine the tortoise bothering him at a time like this.

Her plan had worked, but she wasn't quite finished. She wanted that tortoise gone for good.

She cleared her throat. "Thank you, thank you," she said, like a circus ringleader. "I want to thank Arthur's grandma, and Arthur, too."

More clapping and cheering, then an important sort of silence fell over the hall as she spoke again. "That was my favorite song. It's old and wonderful and I love it because Grandad and I sing it all the time. It's about sticking together and that's what we do."

Grandad nodded as he rubbed his eyes.

"But there's one more old and wonderful thing I want to talk about."

She paused.

All eyes were upon her.

"What is it?" a small voice whispered from the front row.

And Olive said, "It's Grandad."

Heads turned to face the old man at the side of the hall. He sat wide-eyed, his mouth open.

Olive beckoned him to the stage. He unfolded himself out of the chair and strode toward her. Hundreds of captivated faces followed his path as he stepped onto the stage and stood tall and straight beside Olive, his hand on her shoulder. With his skinny chest puffed out, he looked like a proud pigeon wrapping a warm wing around its chick.

"Grandad is my most favorite old and wonderful thing of all," said Olive. "Grandad does everything. He makes my lunch and dinner. He walks me to school. He hugs me before bed and as soon as I wake up. He sings songs and takes me on adventures around town. He teaches me about beautiful birds and paper planes and magical things from long ago like typewriters and record players. And he tells me stories about my mum."

She paused to unfold a piece of paper from her pocket. It had taken her a long time to get these next words right, and she had written them down so she wouldn't forget.

"Grandad rubs out the gray parts of my day and fills them in with color."

At this moment, Grandad swept her up in his scarecrow arms. The crowd cheered, Ms. March blinked away tears, and Arthur's grandma gave the squeeze box a triumphant blast, startling some of the children who had forgotten she was still there.

Wrapped up in her grandfather's arms, Olive looked over his shoulder and watched the old, gray tortoise disappear out the door.

A Falling Sky

The following day, Olive lay on the trampoline, gazing at the pale sky above. It stretched all around like a giant, billowing bedsheet, faded in the sun. She thought of a line from "Side by Side" about the sky falling down. It was supposed to be a bad thing, the end of the world. Looking at the sky now, so light and empty above the town, Olive didn't think a falling sky would hurt very much at all. She didn't think anything could hurt her right now. She had chased away that creaky, old tortoise. She had made Grandad happy.

The feeling of power flooded her body with a tingly sense of joy, until she wriggled and bounced and jumped on the trampoline, higher and higher, much higher than she'd ever jumped before. She spotted the small plant in the gutter on the roof. It shimmered in the afternoon light.

But then she slowed down as she spotted her father wandering home, the elephant plodding beside him.

Since the party, she had pushed them both out of her mind. After all, her father had missed the whole thing. The bike was still broken and now she didn't need it as much as she once had. She had been fine without it.

Without him.

She watched her father and the elephant round the corner of the house and she noticed something. The elephant looked bigger than ever, a great hulking mass, dragging her father down, burying him in its shadow. She watched them both climb the stairs to the house. The steps bent and buckled under their weight.

Just before they disappeared inside, Olive called out. "Dad!"

He turned around. His face was like a pale stone, worn flat by sea and sand. She had never seen him look so sad.

She suddenly wanted to talk and talk, to tell him everything—about the tortoise and

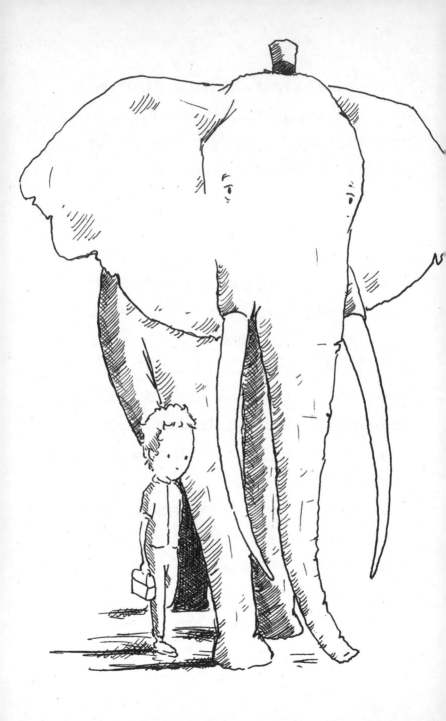

the party, the squeeze box, the paper planes, the colorful pigeon, Ms. March's earrings, and Arthur's books. She longed to share it all and she knew that if she just kept talking they would share secrets to fill more than a cup, more than a river. Bigger than the ocean.

In the end, she said nothing because her father would never listen—*really* listen—with the elephant beside him.

He went into the house.

Olive slid off the trampoline and sat against the trunk of the jacaranda tree. As Freddie snuffled beside her, whimpering and wagging his tail, her voice was calm and strong.

"I'm going to get rid of that elephant."

A Very Big Heart

It was another purple backpack day.

Olive and Grandad stood on the path outside a shop with dusty windows and an old wooden door. The shop was in town, on the edge of the mall. It had taken seven and a half "Side by Sides" to get there.

Grandad fished a water bottle out of his backpack and took a sip. Olive cupped her face against the window and looked into the shop. She couldn't see much through the dust on the glass.

"What is this place?" she asked.

"A second-hand shop," said Grandad. "It's full of old and wonderful things."

"I didn't know it was here," said Olive, brushing dirt off her hands.

"Not many people do, but it's been here for years."

Olive turned to look at him. "Can we go in?" she said.

"Even better," said Grandad. "We're going upstairs, to the very top."

He opened the old wooden door, which groaned as if waking from years of sleep. They stepped inside, into the smell of old timber and musty clothes. They wheeled their heads around to let their eyes soak up the cluttered beauty that surrounded them. Shards of afternoon sunlight angled in through the windows, falling on the piles of odd things that filled every space and every corner.

There were racks of old-fashioned clothes

and towers of battered, brown suitcases. Thin-framed bicycles and kitchen chairs hung from the ceiling. A maze of bookshelves zigzagged toward the far wall. There were desks and beds and boxes of shoes, tables covered with cups and saucepans and teapots. Olive spotted a giant telescope sprouting from the middle of the shop, aimed at a high window.

"This way," whispered Grandad, and she followed him.

As she crept and squeezed her way past so many old and wonderful things, she dreamed up stories for some of them and imagined how

important they had once been to somebody, somewhere, a long time ago.

They reached a narrow, carpeted staircase at the back of the shop, spiraling upward, much further than Olive expected. She watched Grandad's scarecrow legs as she followed him up and up and up until they finally reached a door.

"Here we go," said Grandad, turning the handle.

They were suddenly outside again and were now on top of the shop, standing on the roof. There was a concrete railing all around. Olive leaned over and looked down on the mall as it stretched into the distance. There were no cars, just people moving about. Everybody looked so small as they hurried in and out of the shops.

"We're up very high, Grandad," said Olive.

"We are," he said. "That's why we're here. This is the tallest building in town."

Just as he had done at the cricket oval, he took a piece of paper from the purple backpack. He folded it this way. And that. To make a paper plane.

He cast it off the roof. A breeze lifted the plane higher than their heads. It circled above the mall, swimming through the afternoon air, smooth and silent. Finally, it neared the ground and landed at the feet of a small boy. He picked it up and looked around.

Grandad and Olive ducked behind the

concrete railing. They giggled and gasped with the sort of tingly excitement that overwhelms you when you have just pulled off a trick, something marvelous and secret.

As they hid, Grandad gazed at the milkshake clouds bubbling above the town.

"That was a lovely thing you did for me at the party," he said. "To do something like that, to make an old man so happy—you've got a very big heart."

Olive's body prickled with that same sensation she had felt on the trampoline.

She had an idea.

"Do you have some more paper?" she asked.

She and Grandad made another plane. But before she sent it flying off the roof, she paused.

"Grandad," she said. "Do you have a pen?"

He rummaged in the backpack and found a blue one.

Olive wrote on the plane: *Your hair looks nice.*

She flung it off the roof. It swirled through the air, dipping and diving. At last, it bumped gently into the arm of a lady struggling with a load of shopping bags. The lady put down her bags and picked up the plane. As she unfolded the paper, she glanced around the mall, as if wondering where the plane had come from. Olive and Grandad peered over the edge of the railing and watched.

The lady read the message. Her face brightened and she patted her hair. Once again, she looked around the mall, then carried on with her shopping bags, grinning all the way.

Grandad patted Olive's shoulder. "Let's do another," he said.

As the afternoon stretched on, they sent more and more planes flying off the roof, each with its own message for whoever might find it skidding at their feet.

One of the planes said: *I like your shoes*. Another said: *Look at those purple clouds*. And: *You have a wonderful laugh*.

People picked them up, slightly bewildered at first. Then their faces shone when they read the messages. Nobody seemed to suspect the planes had been launched from the top of the second-hand shop by an old scarecrow and a small girl with a big heart.

The Animals

The two friends wandered home, humming their song and watching the sky turn from blue to orange and yellow and pink, then a rich purple, like the breast of that beautiful pigeon. Olive hopped and twirled beside Grandad. Pictures of the old and wonderful things played in her mind and she felt as light and free as a paper plane floating above the town. This had been her favorite purple backpack day ever.

Perhaps it was the beauty of the sky, perhaps it was the giddiness of the afternoon, but she suddenly felt a compulsion to do something she had never done before, to tell Grandad something she had kept inside for a long time.

She cleared her throat.

"Grandad," she said.

"Hmm?"

"Sometimes I see animals. Big, gray animals. But they're not real."

He didn't flinch. He kept walking as if she had said something quite ordinary about school or dinner.

"What do you mean?" he said.

"Well," she said, "I know the animals aren't really there. I just imagine them, following people around."

"All the time?"

"No," she said. "Only when people are sad. If I see somebody is sad—really sad—I imagine there's a big, gray animal just, you know, hanging around, making everything difficult and heavy."

The two of them waltzed on home. The sky darkened further, and a splatter of stars appeared like pinholes in a curtain.

"Do I have one of these gray animals?" Grandad said.

"You did," said Olive. "When I fell out of the tree you were really sad, so a big tortoise followed you around. But I chased it away."

"How did you do that?"

"I cheered you up," she said. "Remember, at the party?"

The old man smiled and stole a glance at his granddaughter. "Who else?" he said.

Olive fell quiet, but her body twitched and clenched as if something were bursting to get out.

"Your dad? Does he have an animal?"

Olive felt the weight of the question slow

her down. She kicked a pebble as she walked and, for a moment, thought she heard Freddie's bark in the distance.

"Yes," she said, "he does. He has the biggest gray animal of all."

Grandad slowed down so he could keep close beside her. "Because he's so sad?"

Olive nodded. Then she stopped. She stood on the footpath and rolled her head back to look at the dark sky. She hoped it wouldn't fall right now.

"He has an elephant," she said. "A big, gray elephant. I imagine it beside him all the time. It's so big and heavy, and I don't know how I'll ever chase it away."

Grandad bent his scarecrows legs to crouch down beside her.

"Your father has been sad for a long time," he said. "And he might be sad for a bit longer. But it won't be forever."

"It feels like forever," Olive said.

"I know. And I know you chased away the tortoise, but the elephant might be too big for you to move on your own."

Olive gazed again at the night sky and, slowly, an idea began to swirl and take shape in her mind. It started off small, like a star, then it gathered into something bigger and brighter, a cluster of stars, a shimmering constellation.

"Grandad," she said slowly, careful not to let the idea fall to the ground before it ripened. "What if you helped me? What if you helped me chase the elephant away?"

The old man looked down at that small, wise face.

"There's something I should show you," he said. "It's old and wonderful—and I think it might help."

The Shed

Later that night, Olive sat on a stool in Grandad's shed with Freddie by her side. A lightbulb that hung from the ceiling cast a dusty orange glow on all the things stacked around the place. Rusty shovels, teetering piles of pots, an upside-down wheelbarrow missing its wheel. The sweet stench of soil and manure hung thick in the air and Olive heard cockroaches scuttling under the shelves.

"Here it is," said Grandad in a soft, croaky voice.

He reached up to a high shelf, where there

were broken pieces of clay. Perhaps they had come from a cracked pot or a vase. He fumbled with the pieces for a moment, then cradled them down to his workbench. Olive slid off the stool and stood beside him.

She watched as Grandad fit the pieces together and she instantly recognized its shape.

"An elephant," she said. "It's an elephant."

He nodded. It was broken into four or five separate pieces, but joined together by his scarecrow hands, it was beautiful. Everything looked just right—the ears and the trunk and the half-moon toes at the end of each chunky foot. There was a hole on top so you could fill the elephant with soil and use it as a plant pot.

Then she saw something else. Two tiny letters carved into one of the legs.

"Is that—" She ran her fingers over the letters.

"Your mum," Grandad said, putting his arm around her shoulder. "They're her initials."

"But why are they there?"

Freddie pawed at her legs and Grandad squeezed her arm.

"Because she made it," he said, though the words got stuck somewhere in his throat.

A Plan

Olive held the pieces of the elephant in her hands and thought of all the things that had filled her life—both gray and colorful—in the past few months.

The typewriter and the record player. The paper planes and the pigeon. She thought of Freddie and the tortoise. Arthur's books, her mother's old bike, and her father's elephant.

As she looked at the cracked pieces of clay in her hands, a beautiful, broken thing made by her mother, she talked with Grandad.

They talked about her mother. Her father.

And they talked about a plan to get rid of her father's elephant.

Rainbow

There were only a few weeks of school left. Olive told Arthur all about her plan to chase the elephant away. It was an exciting scheme, made up of all the things that Grandad had used to color Olive's life: paper planes, "Side by Side," and some old and wonderful things, too.

"Do you really think it will work?" Arthur asked, peeling a squashed banana. "Do you really think it'll get rid of the elephant?"

Olive bit into her salad wrap.

"I hope so," she said. "I'm sick of it hanging around. So big and heavy and gray."

"Oh!" yelled Arthur, dropping his banana. "That reminds me—I wanted to show you something."

He sprinted toward the classroom and returned a moment later, carrying *The Big Book of Elephants*.

"Look at this!" he said, flipping to a page near the back of the book.

It was a photograph of an elephant that stretched across a double page. The strange thing was, the elephant wasn't gray. It was painted in every bright color imaginable—yellow and green and purple and red, orange and blue and sugary pink. The colors were painted in patterns and swirls, forming leaves and flowers, stars and crescent moons. Sparkling jewelry hung from the elephant's ears and a golden blanket was draped over its back.

"Whoa," she gasped. "That's the most beautiful thing I've ever—"

"They paint them in India," he said. "For a competition." His eyes twinkled and he added something that sounded familiar. "Just goes to show—they're not all gray."

Olive smiled as she remembered the pigeon.

Then it all came together quite simply in her mind: the rainbow elephant, her mother's broken clay, and the plan to cheer up her father.

She couldn't wait.

Chasing the Elephant Away

It was Saturday morning.

Olive peeked through the doorway at her father sleeping, though he was beginning to stir. He rolled slowly to one side and stretched a leg under the sheet. He twitched as a light breeze touched his face and he opened an eye.

A yellow paper plane was tied to the ceiling fan above his bed, spinning around, flying a perfect circle through the air. He smiled, sat up, and found another paper plane resting on his blanket. There was something written on it. He unfolded the paper and Olive knew what

he would see, because she had made it herself.
There were flowers, stars, and birds drawn in
felt pen around the outside of the page and
there was a message in the middle, punched
onto the page by an old typewriter.

Dear Dad

You are invited to breakfast
under the jacaranda tree.

Quick - before the food gets cold!

Love Olive xo

He swung himself out of bed and Olive
tiptoed outside before he could see her. She
waited under the tree with Grandad as her
father opened the back door. He padded down
the steps, stopped on the grass and looked
at the jacaranda. His mouth fell open and a
breathy laugh escaped when he saw hundreds

of colored paper planes hanging from its branches. They twisted and twirled and pirouetted in the breeze. There were purple planes, orange planes, blue, green, yellow, and red.

It was as if the great tree had sprouted flowers of every color: sharp, pointy paper-plane-shaped flowers, flitting and fluttering about.

Under the tree was a small table and chairs, set with plates and cups and a tray of eggs, tomatoes, and toast. Olive and Grandad sat there grinning. Still wearing crumpled pajamas, her father walked over to them.

"This is…lovely," he said.

He sat down and they tucked in. The scrambled eggs warmed Olive's tummy and she looked at what surrounded her: the colorful planes flipping in the breeze above their heads, the soft grass tickling her feet under the table, and, of course, her father.

She watched the morning light color his dry, whiskery, Saturday-morning face. The plan seemed to be working. He certainly looked happy and at that moment she couldn't imagine the elephant anywhere near.

Still, she had to make sure.

She wanted to see the elephant lumber away, disappear, forever.

When their plates had been scraped clean, Olive wiped her mouth with a napkin and offered her hand to her father.

"Dad," she said, trying to remember the exact words Grandad had taught her. "Would you care to dance?"

Her father raised his eyebrows and laughed. Then he wrapped his big, rough hands around her fine fingers and they stood beneath the tree. As if from nowhere, music began to play, soft, tinkling music floating on the air.

Olive's father turned and saw Grandad beside the old record player, in the shade on the grass.

"Is that your record player?" he said. "From upstairs?"

Grandad nodded.

Olive led her father out onto the big lawn. As the record played the first lines of "Side by Side," they began to dance. She held her dad's hand and moved her feet the way Grandad had shown her. It was hard to not step on her dad's toes, but as the song went on she fumbled less and less and bounced smoothly on the grass. She started to giggle as she moved, and Dad laughed, too.

Soon, they were laughing together as they danced all around, circling the trunk of the jacaranda, skipping around the trampoline, dodging the tire swing. The music rang out louder across the yard and Dad picked her up. She squealed as he dipped her upside down. He lifted her high and spun around in dizzying circles. Everything was a breathless blur—the paper planes, the jacaranda flowers, the house, the grass—they all went whirling by in a beautiful haze.

Then the song ended and he slowed down and lowered her to the grass.

"There's one more thing," she said.

She skipped across the yard to Grandad's shed, ducked inside, and then came walking back toward her father, nursing something in her hands.

She held it out as if she were presenting a crown to a new king.

It was her mother's clay elephant and it was no longer broken.

The pieces had been glued back together and purple flowers sprouted from the hole in the top. Her father took it in his heavy hands and ran a finger over the initials on the leg.

"I remember this," he said, turning it around. "But it's much more colorful now."

He was right, because Olive had painted the elephant like a rainbow, with swirly leaves and flowers.

She grinned and said, "They're not all gray, Dad."

He crouched before her, his stubbly face close to hers, and hugged her tight.

"Thank you," he said.

As he squeezed her close, Olive spotted something moving in the yard. It was big and heavy and gray. Her father's elephant.

Olive locked her arms around her father and watched the elephant head off across the grass and out of sight.

It was gone.

The Workshop

On the final day of school, Olive and Arthur wandered toward the gate, making plans to meet up over the holidays.

"I still haven't climbed your tree," said Arthur.

"And I want a go on that squeeze box," said Olive.

They reached the gate and Olive threw her arms around Grandad.

"Hello, love," he said.

Her face shone as she noticed his purple backpack.

They bounced along the footpath, singing "Side by Side." By the time they had sung it seven times, they had reached an industrial street outside of town. It was full of sheds and machinery and rumbling trucks.

They stopped outside a mechanic's garage.

"This looks like Dad's workshop," said Olive. The office door was shut and the big metal roller door was down. "But...where is he?"

"He...um..." Grandad scratched his wispy white hair. "He's somewhere else right now. But he wanted me to show you something."

He lifted the roller door and they stepped inside. It smelled of gasoline and paint. Dirty rags were strewn about the place and somebody's car sat in the middle of the workshop. Its hood was open, exposing greasy, metal insides, like a patient on an operating table.

Grandad flicked a switch and the workshop lit up.

Olive saw the walls and her heart nearly stopped.

They were covered with photographs of her: Olive as a baby, Olive starting school, Olive on the trampoline, Olive leaping over a crashing wave at the beach. There were school photos, holiday photos and blurry nothing-much-at-all photos. In between the pictures, there were drawings that she had scribbled, from her early scrawls to recent sketches. There was hardly a spare spot on the walls.

"Has it always been like this?" she said.

Grandad nodded. "For years and years."

As she staggered around the workshop, staring at the gallery, Olive realized why Grandad had brought her here today. He was sharing a secret. He had peeled back a curtain to show how her father really felt about her, how much he loved her. All this time, she hadn't looked past his elephant and its big, gray shadow. Now that it was gone, she could see the light that was hiding the whole time. She felt as if she had been lifted above the surface of the water, to see the whole ocean, full of the secrets her father kept inside.

It was a wonderful feeling, but as she looked around the workshop, her smile fell away.

"My bike's not here," she mumbled, turning to Grandad. "And—where *is* Dad anyway?"

He arched his eyebrows and patted his backpack.

"There's one more surprise," he said.

The Surprise

When Olive arrived home, she spotted Freddie circling and panting on the top step. She started toward him, but Grandad took her hand.

"This way," he said with a wrinkly smile.

He covered her eyes with his old hands and led her around the side of the house. Freddie scurried down the steps and trotted beside them. They reached the backyard and edged toward the jacaranda tree.

"Are you ready?" said Grandad.

Olive nodded.

He took his hands away.

"Ohhh!" she gasped.

Her breath escaped in shaky, excited bursts, because in front of her was a bike, shining in the afternoon sun.

It was her bike.

Her mother's.

She leaned closer and ran her fingers along the frame and the stitching of the padded seat. She pinched the tires, squeezed the handlebar grips and rang the bell.

Ding!

Just like the old typewriter.

She stood up. "The bike's here," she wondered aloud. "But where's Dad?"

"Up here."

The voice had come from overhead. A deep voice.

She looked up into the branches of the jacaranda and there he was.

Her father.

He was sitting on one of the thicker limbs, holding a sleek, white paper plane in his hands, grinning down at her.

"Dad!" she squealed. "What are you doing up there?"

"Watch this," he said, ignoring her question. "I worked out how to make them."

He flung the plane out of the tree. It cut a graceful curve through the air, then spiraled smoothly to land on the grass.

Olive beamed up at her father. Her heart drummed like butterfly wings and her hands shook.

Was this really happening?

Was she dreaming?

No, perhaps this was just what it felt like when wishes came true. Her father had climbed the tree. He had made a paper plane. Fixed the bike.

All of these things had been impossible when the elephant was still around.

"Come on, then," said Dad, jumping down from the branches. "Have a ride."

Grandad pulled her helmet out of the purple backpack. She strapped it on and gripped the handlebars, threw one foot onto a pedal and pushed off the grass with the other. The tires wove a wobbly line along the grass. Then she pedaled faster and rode smooth rings around the whole yard, lapping the trampoline and the tree. She rode faster, splitting the wind. She felt as if she were flying, like a perfectly folded plane soaring through the afternoon sky.

As she rode around and around, she heard cheers and clapping from the two grown-ups standing in the middle of the grass, and that familiar tingly feeling sparkled inside her. She had chased away their gray animals.

She knew Grandad was right. They might

still feel sad sometimes. But the tortoise was gone. The elephant, too.

It was then that Olive slowed down and stopped the bike.

There was one more animal that had still been hanging around.

One more she hadn't told anybody about, but had kept to herself.

A small, gray dog with short legs and an extra-long tail.

Good-bye

Olive rested the bike on the grass and walked around the side of the house to the front gate, where the others couldn't see her. She imagined Freddie sitting at the gate, wagging that long tail of his and looking up at her.

She crouched down and cuddled him close. He licked her face. A single tear slid down her cheek and Freddie licked that, too. They had shared these moments so many times— whenever Olive had fallen or cried or thought of the mother she had never known, whenever she was lost or lonely or just plain sad. In these moments, she had always imagined Freddie snuffling, whimpering, keeping close, keeping her warm.

Now, as much as she loved him, she knew she wouldn't need him anymore. She was happy and strong enough for life without him.

She whispered into his furry ear.

"Everything's okay," she said. "You can go now."

She squeezed him one more time and then let go. She pictured him turn and trot away down the footpath, his tail held high.

The soft image grew smaller and smaller, until, finally, he was gone.

Perfect

The next morning, Olive and Dad lay on the trampoline, watching the leaves of the jacaranda swish and sway above their heads. Grandad was stomping around the pumpkin patch, picking grasshoppers off the big, furry leaves.

Dad wore his stubbly Saturday-morning face and Olive stroked his prickly chin as she talked.

She told him all about the old and wonderful things at school.

She told him about the beautiful pigeon

and throwing paper planes off the second-hand shop.

She even told him about the gray animals.

Dad lay still and listened as the stories flowed. She had held them in for so long and now she could let them out, like caged birds sweeping up into the bright sky.

When she had finished, he squeezed her hand. "You know, I was thinking that perhaps we should get an animal of our own," he said. "A real one, I mean."

"A pet?" Olive sprang up onto her knees.

She dreamed up all sorts of exotic pets.

"Could we get a giraffe?" she said. "An orangutan?"

Dad frowned.

"What about a penguin?" she said, bouncing on her knees. "A toucan? Meerkat? A baby panda?"

Dad scruffed up her hair and laughed.

"Slow down, slow down," he said. "Why don't we start with a dog and think about pandas later."

"Okay," she said, lying back down.

"The first thing we'll need to do is think of a name," he said. "Can you think of a good name for a dog?"

Olive snuggled into her father's side. She closed her eyes and thought of her old friend, her small, gray dog with the short legs and that extra-long tail.

"Yes," she said. "I've got a name that'll be perfect."

Acknowledgments

I'm so proud that this book has my name on it, but it should have many more. I didn't really do it alone.

Thank you to Kristina Schulz, for believing in this story from the very start, when I shakily handed you my early chapters and mumbled the idea that was still growing in my head. I'm so grateful for the attention you have given this little book.

To Kristy Bushnell, thank you for spotting all the tiny things that slipped me by, for crying in all the right spots, and for keeping me to schedule. I'd still be drawing elephants if it wasn't for you.

Thanks to Mark MacLeod, who turns editing into a beautiful art. You helped me polish this story into something much brighter than I ever imagined. I enjoyed reading your corrections so much that I almost wanted more. Almost.

Huge thanks to Jo Hunt for a wonderful design and for tolerating my indecision about the cover.

To the entire UQP team, thanks for having me on board and for supporting your writers so well.

Thank you to Allison Paterson, who gave me a huge boost of encouragement after reading an early draft.

To Mum and Dad and the whole family, thanks for your love and support.

To Bron, Sophie and Elizabeth—it might be odd having a husband and dad who daydreams about imaginary elephants and tortoises all day, but when I'm not doing that, I'm usually thinking about how lucky I am to have you. Just like Olive's grandad, you rub out the gray parts of my day and fill them in with color.

And finally, to Georgie, our small, gray dog with short legs and an extra-long tail, who recently grew too old for this world. You always knew when an elephant came near, and how to chase it away.

Peter Carnavas writes and illustrates books for children and the grown-ups in their lives. His first book, *Jessica's Box*, was shortlisted for the Queensland Premier's Literary Award and the CBCA Crichton Award for Emerging Illustrators. He has since created many books, including *Last Tree in the City*, *The Children Who Loved Books* and *Blue Whale Blues*. He has also illustrated Damon Young's series of humorous picture books that celebrate family diversity. He is a popular presenter in schools and his work has been translated into many languages, including Italian, Portuguese, Korean and Dutch. Peter lives on the Sunshine Coast with his wife, two daughters and a small, charming dog called Florence.

www.petercarnavas.com